KT-574-265

Ghostscape

Joe Layburn

Illustrated by John Williams

F

FRANCES LINCOLN
CHILDREN'S BOOKS

BOMBS AND BULLIES

When this all started I was just a girl in a headscarf in a strange new world. I've seen war, dead bodies too, but you don't see ghosts every day. Not even in Somalia.

"You're making it up," the girls in my class complained. But how could I? I knew nothing about history – not English history anyway – when I first came to this land of rain and snow, and when I first saw a ghost I could reach out and touch. Well, first he touched me – and I'm happy now that he did.

★ ★ ★

I was crying and I'd locked myself in one of the

toilet cubicles. The place stank. Girls were always saying, "Miss, can I go toilet?" to get out of lessons, but believe me, you wouldn't want to spend any longer than you had to in there.

Outside, I heard a cough. I thought they must have sent Fadimo because they always did when I got upset. It was a pain to Fadimo because she didn't want to be Somali or speak our language at school any more. "What is your *problem?*" she would hiss.

My dad's dead, my mum doesn't understand me, I'm being bullied – where do you want me to start?

But it wasn't Fadimo. I opened the cubicle door, my eyes bleary with tears. It was a boy. A boy in our toilet! Sometimes they'd get dragged in by a gang of the noisy, flirty girls from Year Six. But this one just stood there. I didn't recognize him.

"Blimey, look at you!" he said. He stretched out a pale hand and touched my headscarf just above my left eye. "What the hell have you got on your head?"

I actually laughed. It wasn't as if I was an unusual sight — there were lots of girls like me who kept their heads covered. He didn't sound like he was being unkind though. He seemed genuinely amazed.

"You know you shouldn't be here?" he said. "Dickie-bird'll kill you."

"Who's Dickie-bird?"

It was his turn to look baffled. "Dickinson. Mr Dickinson, the Headmaster."

It seemed this boy was mad or had emotional problems or something, because our head teacher wasn't called Dickinson and she wasn't a man either.

"What's your name?" he asked.

"Aisha." I just said it. I was having a conversation with a boy in the girls' toilets. So?

He was wearing shorts, but not like PE shorts. These were grey and hung down to below his knees. He had a grimy white shirt with a big collar and scuffed black shoes as well, but it was the spiral of curls on top of his head that I noticed most. His hair was cropped close at the sides but up above it was crazy like spaghetti.

"You don't say much, Aisha," he said with a wink. "Are you scared? Of the bombs? They scare me all right, I don't mind telling you. Boom, boom, boom." He chuckled, then coughed.

"I hate even thinking about the sound of guns," I said.

"Is that what you was crying about?"

I shook my head. "Do you know Chevon?" I asked.

He screwed up his nose, which was speckled with orangey freckles. "I thought I knew everyone in this school, but I don't know you and I've never heard of Chevon. What class?"

I waved in the vague direction of my classroom, but, for the first time, I noticed that things around me weren't right. The walls, which until now had been painted snot-green, were covered in shiny white tiles. The sinks were different too and the door to the corridor was in the wrong place. One of the taps was dripping incredibly loudly – the sound echoed faster and faster. I felt frightened and dizzy.

"Are you ill or something?" the boy asked. "You look like you've seen a ghost."

That's when the floor seemed to lurch up and hit me on the side of the head. Next I was falling through blackness and when I opened my eyes again, the pale, blond boy was gone and I was back in the girls' toilets of Trentham Primary School.

★ ★ ★

The first person I saw when I got back to class was Chevon. She was just inside the door, waiting. Everyone else had stampeded out for break. Taller than me, older looking, Chevon wore make-up even though girls at school were not supposed to.

"Miss said she couldn't hang around any longer for you," she explained when she saw me peering past her in search of Miss Brown. Chevon – pronounced Sheh-*von* – used a thumbnail to tease out a drawing pin that was stuck in the pockmarked wall.

"You're well out of order, Aisha. I'm going to get you for what you did to me."

"What did I do?" I protested, angry but fearful.

"You know what you did." She flicked the drawing pin at me. "You cussed my mum."

"Oh, Chevon, I never. I'd never say anything bad about your mum."

"You're evil, you are."

"Chevon, can't you just leave me alone?"

Her eyes widened. "Why should I? Witch!"

She came to slap me and though I saw the blow coming and ducked, it caught me in the mouth.

"Urrrrr, you spat on me. You cow," she said, pushing me hard against the door.

"Stop that! Both of you. I won't stand for it. You should be ashamed of yourselves."

It was Mr Franks, a fat, wheezy supply teacher with a grey goatee beard, who waddled around the school in a mist of bad breath. I could smell it now – a dead animal rotting.

"What kind of example is this for younger children?" he added, though there were no younger children around. "I'm giving you three days' detention. Both of you. No arguments."

"But, sir, she cussed my mum," Chevon said. "I've got a right to defend myself and my family if someone cusses them."

Mr Franks looked uncertain. He wasn't entirely stupid and he knew something of Chevon's tricks.

"And then the dirty cow spat at me, sir."

Mr Franks turned to inspect me. "What do you have to say for yourself?"

"Nothing, sir."

"In that case, you can have four days' detention. If you won't even think about what you've done wrong, you give me no choice."

"And she tried to jack my pencil case, sir," Chevon added.

Mr Franks looked quizzically at Chevon. The suspicion was apparently growing within him that he was being taken for a fool. "Did you try to steal Chevon's pencil case, er...?"

I realised he couldn't remember my name. "Aisha," I said. "No I never."

"Don't push me too far, Chevon," he muttered. "Now go out and play."

Chevon brushed past me, head held high. "Shame," she said loudly.

I sought refuge in a corner of the playground under a skinny dead tree with Leyla and Sufia. About twenty boys were playing football, all shrieking "pass it, man!" at Sufia's big brother

Omar. But he played like he was possessed, never looking up to pass to anyone. The other kids couldn't understand how he'd picked up their game so quickly. Of course, in Somalia, he would have run around in a cloud of dust with a ball at his feet any chance he'd had. He didn't let on to these boys though.

Gooaal, he shouted, a flash of white teeth, proud brown eyes, a glance towards where we were standing. Leyla and I smiled shyly, but he ignored us. Typical.

I was telling Leyla and Sufia about the boy in the toilets.

"I reckon you was seeing things cos you're so stressed out by Chevon," Leyla said.

I picked at the bark of the dead tree. "I was talking to him like I'm talking to you."

I noticed that Sufia was getting her spacey look that meant she was about to say something weird.

"I see giant helicopters sometimes, coming through smoke. Their noise fills my head and

I want to scream."

No disrespect to Sufia, but Omar, her brother, reckoned she got a lot of this stuff from a Hollywood war film about Somalia called *Black Hawk Down*. Their uncle said it made Somalis look like wild animals. He got even more upset about a video game version of *Black Hawk Down*. Western children would be blasting away at evil Somalis in their bedrooms, he said – kerpow, pow, pow. It made their uncle so miserable he pulled bits of his beard out. Seriously.

Poor Sufia was not right in the head either. Under our tree, Leyla and I made some soothing, pigeon style noises, just to show we were paying attention, then we got back to my story – my ghost.

"Was he fit, Aisha? You say he's got hair like spaghetti – what else?"

"Leyla, this was basically a very scary moment. Not like a Romeo and Juliet thing."

Leyla made a face as if to say *Who?* But I knew

she knew because Miss Brown had shown us some parts of a film with Leonardo DiCaprio as Romeo because it was "artistic and beautiful" even though it "wasn't exactly age-appropriate".

"I feel like I will see him again," I said.

"So it is a Romeo and Juliet thing." Leyla giggled. "You and Mister Spaghetti-Head are star-crossed lovers."

I started to laugh too but then a cloud passed across the sun and I suddenly felt cold. From nowhere, Chevon had appeared.

"You got a lover then, Aisha? I didn't think Somali girls was allowed to have boyfriends or nothing." Chevon stood with one hand on a hip, chin jutting out at me.

"I wasn't talking to you, Chevon."

I stepped away from the muddy base of the tree on to the cracked concrete of the playground.

"You're talking to me now and you can show me some respect."

"OK, I respect you. I'll give you respect.

Whatever."

"I asked you a question."

"Chevon, Miss Brown said she couldn't make us all be best friends but we had to get along together. That's all I want."

"That's just circle-time talk, innit? I don't have to get along with no one. Ain't no one going to tell me what to do."

"Chevon, I wouldn't try to tell you anything. You're bigger than me."

"You saying I'm fat? You diss my mum and now you tell me I'm fat?"

"I didn't say that."

A strange smile animated Chevon's sullen, pouting features. "What if, Aisha yeah, what if I tell your mum you've got a boyfriend? I bet it's Omar? What if I tell your mum that I seen you with Omar?"

This I feared far more than physical hurt. Would Chevon really approach my mum and say something about me and a boy? I thought that she might and it made me tremble.

"Just don't. Please. Don't."

"Stop me."

I'm not proud of this next bit.

I tried to slap her around the head, but she leaned backwards and I found myself clawing at her neck instead. Her skin was moist with sweat but not so slick that I couldn't dig in and hold on with my fingernails. I yanked her downwards. She writhed and shrieked at me to let go. But how could I? I had to keep her there. I had to grasp this slippery fold of skin until the broken nails on my fingers were snagged in it like fish hooks. She was hunched over on the uneven surface of the playground now, head bent as though in prayer. Her screams were truly awful. But how could I let her go?

I closed my eyes and my ears filled with the sound of her wailing. It was then that I felt his hand resting gently on my wrist.

"We've got to go, Aisha. That's the sirens going off. We're in danger."

The wailing sound no longer seemed to come

from Chevon's throat. It was mechanical but not like the electric scream of police cars. This was deeper, a ghostly yowling as if to announce the end of the world.

"I can't go," I said, my eyes still screwed shut, my hand clenched, holding on to my tormentor.

"We've got to leave. You should see the damage they done in my street last night. There was nothing left of this one house but a pile of bricks with a bathtub sitting on the top. It looked quite comical in a way, but the people that lived there was all dead."

I opened one eye.

"Look, I don't know who you are, but I'm staying here and this evil witch is staying with me."

I looked down at my right hand. Across the palm was a jagged line of blood oozing from four gouges I had made with my fingernails.

"There ain't no evil witches," the boy said. "Just Hitler and his Nazi bombers."

As he spoke I felt the ground shake. It was as

if a lorry had been dropped from the top of the block of flats down the road from the school. But that particular tower block hadn't been built yet. My class wouldn't be learning about the Second World War until Year Six, but I was starting to get the idea of what was happening here. Chevon was gone, so was the modern version of my school, which had been replaced by a soaring Victorian building of sooty bricks and tall windows. *Trentham Primary* it said high on one wall in flowery old writing. The name was the same, but as I looked around I could see so much that was different.

"Some quick questions," I said, as the air raid sirens continued to wail. "Just answer them, then we can go."

The boy looked dubious, but he nodded.

"What's your name?"

"Richard."

"What year is this?"

"1940."

"Do you know somewhere we'll be safe?"

"I think so."

"Then let's get out of here."

The ground shook again. He took my hand in his and we ran.

I'm Invisible!

We sheltered, breathless, under an arch of a railway bridge. The sound of the bombs as they crashed upon the shuddering earth was not just something I experienced with my ears – my face tingled, my legs trembled, my insides seemed to be dragged down towards my feet. For a few seconds, my whole body was possessed by the noise.

Looking back the way we had run, I saw more planes, like a flock of huge silver birds droning towards us. They glinted in the pale sunlight, their wings spread wide. Just across the street I could see the destruction they would bring.

The whole front of some poor family's home had been ripped away leaving the rooms and staircase exposed like a doll's house. I almost felt ashamed to see their personal things: the wallpaper they had chosen, a woman's lilac dressing gown still hanging behind her bedroom door. There was debris and broken glass everywhere, but the mirror of her dressing table was still in one piece, as though she might yet brush out her hair in front of it before settling down for the night.

We huddled together under the arch, his arm around my shoulders. Water was seeping through the blackened red bricks above my head and splashing down on to the ground beside me. I could also hear the chattering of gunfire from a few streets away.

"Those guns sound close, Richard."

"They're ours. Ack ack guns. To me they don't seem to do no good at all, like gnats attacking a rhinoceros. But I suppose it shows we're putting up a fight."

"In Somalia the bad guys used to ride in jeeps firing off bullets into the sky, into people's homes. They'd be whooping and shouting. It seemed like a game to them."

"So British Somaliland is where you're from?"

Despite everything I smiled. British Somaliland was a really old-fashioned name for part of my country. It hadn't been called that for years. "Yeah, but I'm never going back."

"Good for you, Aisha. Once the war's over, this country'll be a great place for everyone. If it ain't been bombed completely flat that is."

"It doesn't bother you that I'm different?"

"As far as I'm concerned, we're all in this together," Richard said. "Bombs'll land on you just the same as me. It don't matter you're a different colour – or that you've got a towel round your head."

I pinched his arm. "It's called a hijab...," I started to say, but the planes were almost upon us now and the words caught in my throat.

"You really reckon this place is safe?" I whispered finally.

He shrugged. "It ain't perfect. And if they

score a direct hit we're done for. But there's plenty of people use railway arches. And after spending a night in a public shelter I ain't never going back to one. There was people singing all sorts of soppy songs all night long. Little kids whimpering and crying cos of nightmares. And worst of all was the stink. Pretty much everyone had a dicky stomach and them that weren't trumping all night, like some big brass band, were fighting over the toilets so they could dump their load."

I giggled nervously.

"Where are the rest of your family, Richard?"

"It's just me and me grandad and he refuses to leave the house whatever's happening outside. He pulls the bedclothes over his head and stays there till they sound the All Clear. He won't even sleep under the kitchen table, which I've told him would be better than nothing cos it's downstairs and he'd have a bit more protection. He just says when your number's up, your number's up. The last war took years off him, he reckons, and he ain't getting out of bed for this one at all."

Suddenly a tremor went through the arch where we were sheltering and my ears were filled with the roar of a massive explosion: it seemed to suck all other sounds out of the air. Bits of masonry began falling and we were showered with rubble and dust.

Instinctively, I started to run. Richard tried to pull me back. He was shouting but it was as if we were underwater. I could see his mouth moving but nothing audible was coming out. I felt my way along the wall and peered into the adjoining street. There was a crater as long as a bus. Three houses in a terrace were in flames and there seemed to be pieces of burning paper and clothing swirling and dancing in the hot air. As my hearing returned, I could hear the mad yapping of a terrified dog echoing further down the road.

"You silly moo. Will you get yourself back here?"

The dust had started to settle and I could see that our railway arch was still standing pretty much as before. Richard looked wide-eyed and paler than ever. There was a smudge of dirt on his right cheek but he seemed to be unharmed.

"You all right?" he asked.

"Just a bit shaken."

As I stumbled across the fallen rubble towards him, an air raid warden in a tin hat appeared from the other side of the arch. His round face was red, as if it had been boiled and he had a pencil-thin grey moustache above blubbery lips.

"You still in one piece?" he wheezed.

"We're fine," Richard told him. "Never been better."

"What d'you mean *we*?" the warden asked, looking around. He looked right through me and I realised with an icy shiver that I was invisible to him. I walked right up to him, so close that I could have flicked the tip of his nose with a finger. I shook my head to and fro, stuck my tongue out, rolled my eyes, but he simply looked straight over my shoulder at Richard, his eyebrows raised.

"I mean me and her," Richard said.

He pointed in my direction, but the air raid warden simply spun round and looked behind him.

"I'm talking about Aisha here," Richard said, perplexed. "My mad mate from Somaliland."

The air raid warden's eyebrows dropped down now and knitted together into a frown. "Don't be fooling with me, sunshine. There's a war on, in case you hadn't noticed."

"He can't see me!" I squealed. "Only you can,

Richard."

I reached up and flipped the air raid warden's tin hat so that it fell off his head and landed with a clatter at his feet.

"Oi!" he shouted, spinning around again and almost losing his footing on the loose rubble underneath his black boots. "What the bleeding hell's going on?"

Richard stifled a laugh with his hand.

"Nothing's going on," he said. "Look, there's only me here and I'm as happy as a sandboy."

The air raid warden picked up his helmet, dusted it down and stamped off the way he had come.

"Oh, Richard," I said taking his hands in mine and spinning him around as though we were dancing partners. "I thought you were my ghost. But it seems I'm yours too."

I felt lightheaded as we scampered through the

darkening streets to where Richard lived. He was anxious to check on his grandad, of course. Some of the houses we passed were just piles of bricks and rags. In others, treasured ornaments were still on a mantelpiece, or a table had been laid for a meal, but the rest of the room was gone. There were lonely-looking staircases that pointed up into the sky and groaning bedroom floors that sagged down towards the rooms below. Torn curtains flapped in the wind through empty window frames. Everywhere was the smell of smoke and the crackling sound of fire.

We arrived to find Richard's grandad wrapped in a blanket, his wild white hair full of dust and grit, leaning on the gatepost and looking ruefully at the smoking mountain of rubble and broken furniture that had once been his home.

Many houses in the street had simply collapsed under the reverberations of a bomb that had set the nearby church ablaze; flames licked around a metal cross on top of the spire, while grey slates crashed down from the roof.

The sun seemed to be setting in the east today because fires at the docks had turned the sky a coppery orange.

Many of Richard's neighbours were milling around in the street. Some carried bundles of clothing and food. Others had rescued things that were dear to them: a silver framed photograph of a uniformed father away at the front; a wooden toy tank painted army green; a yellow canary in a metal cage. It was clear that many more Nazi bombers would be back that night – their path guided by the burning homes and factories that the fire brigade were powerless to put out.

The people standing around me needed shelter; they were frightened and uncertain. I saw one mother absent-mindedly stroking her daughter's long black hair and I realized that she was doing it to comfort herself as much as her little girl. I knew that bewildered look. I had seen it on the face of my own mother when we were forced to flee our home in Somalia.

These people were refugees now and I knew all about refugees.

Two air raid wardens appeared, one an old man with no front teeth, the other a red-haired boy who looked no more than fifteen. The older man whistled when he spoke. He seemed nervous about talking to such a large group of people.

"Listen up folks. They've found a place where you can stay, those of you as have got no homes. You're to go to Trentham School. There's already a big crowd there, so if you want a decent spot to bed down for the night you'd best get over there."

Richard's grandad looked doubtful. "So they want me to go back to school now, do they?" he asked.

Richard squeezed the old man's arm. "I don't see there's much choice. You can't stay here and a railway arch is no good for you, out in the cold all night."

His grandad made the kind of face you see on

little children when they want a sweet or some other treat. "Will you come with me, Rich?"

It was the grandson's turn to look dubious. "They'll be trying to evacuate all the kids that go there now, I know they will. I don't want to leave London. I need to stay here and keep an eye on you."

"I won't let them send you anywhere, Rich. Come with me. I'm not going on my own."

I felt really worried about all this. We'd been outside the school when the bombs started falling earlier that day and it wasn't like it was protected or reinforced or anything. Still, if that's what the authorities were insisting, what could Richard, or his grandad or anyone do?

When we arrived, the school was in chaos. Mothers were nursing babies in the classrooms and corridors. Whenever one child started crying, all the others began howling too. There were sums chalked up on a blackboard; it seemed they'd still been teaching lessons until recently, but now there were blankets and mattresses everywhere and half-dressed people, many of them elderly. Five relentlessly cheerful women were rushing around with mugs of tea and hastily-made corned beef sandwiches. A man with his face covered in bandages was slumped against a wall singing in a low, monotone voice.

"Will you shut your bleeding row, or you're getting no tea from me?" one of the volunteer workers called over to him. He ignored her and carried on his mournful song.

"Well it ain't exactly the Ritz," Richard's grandad said.

"And you ain't paying Ritz prices," said a volunteer who was passing by with a fistful of tea mugs. "D'you want one of these? A cup of tea makes most things better."

Richard's grandad took a mug and thanked her. "Are you staying then?" he asked Richard when she'd bustled off.

Richard sighed, raised his hands in the air then let them fall to his sides. "I'm staying."

The two of them found a spot in the corner of a classroom away from the windows. Richard's grandad lay down on his back, still wrapped in his blanket and, within minutes, was asleep, grunting, spluttering and snoring like an old dog. Richard and I sat down next to him with our backs against the cold tiles of the wall.

"Maybe they won't come back tonight," I whispered.

Richard looked so weary, as if he hadn't slept in days. "They'll be back. They haven't finished the job yet."

I rested my head against his shoulder.

"Tell me about this Chevon," he said.

"Chevon?"

"The one who upset you."

I looked up at the ceiling. There was an ugly crack across part of it shaped like a fork of lightning. "She doesn't seem such a big deal now."

"Still, if she upset you."

"She's just in my face all the time. I've tried to understand why she does it."

Richard clenched and unclenched a fist as if he was squeezing a tennis ball. "You can't give in to bullies. Whatever they do and however much they upset you, you mustn't give in. Just like with Hitler. He's the biggest bully of them all but we've got to stand up to him. He can knock down all our houses, but he can't get rid of all of us. One day we'll sort him out, I promise you."

I smiled and shook my head. "Chevon's not in that league, Richard. She's pretty pathetic when I think about it. Just a schoolgirl with issues."

"Don't let her get you down, Aisha. You're worth more than that."

I liked that. He was right, I was worth something. I fell asleep, leaning against him, still with a smile on my face.

CHEVON, MEET RICHARD

I woke up in my own bed aching all over.

"You fainted," my mum told me as I blinked my sleep-gummed eyes open and saw her round face peering down at me, anxious as usual. "You were fighting with a girl and you fainted."

Still groggy, I carefully explored a bruised area on the back of my head with the tips of my fingers. Ouch!

"You banged your head," my mum said.

I opened my right hand and examined my palm. The wound was scabbing over.

"Also from fighting," my mum explained. "Why do you have to make such trouble?"

I shifted round on to one elbow so that I could see her better. The sun was streaming in through grimy net curtains. "I've got to stick up for myself, Mum. I can't be pushed around by that girl any more."

My mum made this deep tutting sound that she makes. "You hurt her very badly. They are talking about suspending you both from school. Miss Brown has taken your side, though. She says you must have been provoked to do what you did."

My head was throbbing and the sunlight was hurting my eyes.

"Did you eat properly yesterday?" my mum asked.

"I think I did."

She picked at the stitching on my duvet. "You must eat properly, Aisha. And I know that you're not sleeping properly either."

"What makes you say that?"

"Sometimes I hear you moaning and calling out. Other times I come in here and you're staring at the ceiling. Are you dreaming about your father?"

"Maybe. Look, I don't know. What time is

it anyway?"

"Don't change the subject, girl."

"No, seriously. I've got to get to school so that I can talk to Miss Brown about the Second World War."

My mum frowned and shook her head. "Haven't we had enough war? I'm sure that's what your poor father would say if he was here."

I swung my legs out of the bed and gingerly stood up. "This is really important, Mum. I've got to find out about the Nazis and bombers, and the people who lived round here in 1940."

My mum looked doubtful. "First it was crying all the time at school, now it's fighting."

"I'm not going to get in trouble today. I promise. But Mum, I've got to go."

"You must eat some breakfast first," she snapped.

"Once I've eaten my breakfast," I said.

She watched in silence as I ate three spoonfuls of porridge and half a banana. Then she made that tutting sound again.

Whatever! I thought as I slammed the front door shut behind me.

★ ★ ★

I signed in late at the school office and skirted round the big hall, avoiding the bedlam of an infant PE lesson. I crossed the playground where the older children were on break and climbed up to 5A's classroom. The steps were wet from a cloudburst of rain and the windows were fogged with condensation.

Miss Brown was usually here at breaktime. She was small with straightened black hair scraped back in a ponytail and big eyes that were always smiley apart from when she was trying to reason with some of the more difficult children. Then she looked so sad and serious, you wondered if she was actually going to cry. I'm making her sound weak, which she wasn't. She just seemed to care a great deal about all the children, even the ones who spent the whole lesson trying to mess up the things she'd planned for us to do.

I knocked on the door and heard a voice say *Enter*. But it wasn't Miss Brown, it was Chevon. Despite my brave talk about standing up to her, I began to tremble.

"Why don't you come in, Aisha? We got lots to talk about."

Here we go again, I thought.

"You were so out of order, yesterday, Aisha. I ain't going to forgive you. I don't care if they expel me. I'm going to hunt you down, in school or out of school. I showed my sisters what you done to my neck and they said they're comin' here from senior school to have a word with you. This ain't over, Aisha. Believe me."

I was angry as usual, frightened as usual. But suddenly my mood lifted, because, just behind Chevon, there appeared a pale, skinny boy with curly blond hair and a devilish look on his face.

I laughed out loud.

"You got some front," said Chevon, scowling, oblivious to the ghostly figure now beside her.

I laughed again because I saw that he was holding a piece of chalk in his hand. He flicked it at Chevon and it pinged against her right ear.

"Oi!" she squealed, before looking with some surprise at the piece of chalk that had fallen at her feet. "How did you do that?"

She hadn't seen the half of it. Richard walked slowly across the classroom and began examining the class globe. He found Africa, then Somalia and pointed at it, grinning. Chevon turned slowly to see what I was looking at. I, of course, saw Richard lift the globe carefully off the counter and walk solemnly towards her. But since he was invisible to Chevon, all she could see was an inanimate object hovering slowly towards her.

"Oh my God!" she shrieked.

Richard threw the globe at her. She ducked just in time and it crashed against the blackboard.

Next he reached for a flowerpot on Miss Brown's desk that contained a leathery green succulent. I shook my head. Miss Brown loved this ugly-looking plant. But there was no stopping him. Again, Chevon saw it rise up from the desk, then hurl itself across the classroom at her. Her eyes were wide with fear and she was whimpering like a puppy.

"Seen enough yet?" I roared at her.

"Just stop, please, Aisha. Whatever you're doing please make it stop."

"You reckoned I was a witch, Chevon. Want to see what else I can do?"

The board rubber flew across the room, followed by some paint brushes.

"Please stop. I'll never do nothing to you again. I promise."

The strip lights above our heads were flickering on and off as Richard fooled with the switches on the wall.

"Aisha, for God's sake stop it! I'm sorry I was mean. I'm sorry I said that stuff about you and Omar. You got to stop this."

"Chevon," I said, "you are a weak, pathetic bully. Don't you dare bother me or anybody else again. If you do, you'll see some real fireworks. Understand?"

She nodded, clearly terrified.

"And you won't tell no one about this, will you Chevon? I'll know if you do."

She shook her head vigorously.

"Now get out of here, before I chuck the tables and chairs at you."

Trust me, you have never seen anyone make a quicker getaway. She skidded across the carpet tiles, flung the classroom door open and jumped down the flight of steps outside. I moved to the window, wiped away some of the condensation, and watched her gallop like a bolting horse across the playground.

"Thank you. Thank you so much," I said to Richard, who was laughing so hard the tears were running down his face. I grabbed the dustpan and brush from under Miss Brown's desk and began scooping up the soil from the plant pot.

"That was amazing," I said, my heart beating

fast, my head as light as a balloon. I glanced up to see if he had managed to compose himself, but Richard had disappeared – gone as suddenly as he'd come.

By the time Miss Brown came back to the classroom, I'd cleared everything away: the globe was back on the counter, the ugly plant squatting once more on the corner of her desk. She pushed the door open with her foot, labouring under a teetering pile of books. She must have been concerned about the incident in the playground the day before, but she managed a smile for me, her brown eyes all twinkly.

"How are you, Aisha? I wasn't really expecting you today. Do you want to talk about what happened?"

She placed the books carefully on a chair.

"There's actually something else I'd like to talk about first if that's OK."

"Go on," she said, nodding.

"I'd really like to find out more about the Second World War and what happened in this area."

Miss Brown was nodding even more enthusiastically now. "Well, we will have to discuss the Chevon situation at some point, Aisha, and Mrs Greening will want to see you in her office too, but, since everyone's at games now and I very much doubt you're feeling up to that, I suppose we could have a chat about the War."

She indicated for me to sit down next to her at one of the tables.

"Did you know, Aisha, that two and a half million Asians, 375,000 Africans and many thousands of West Indians fought for Britain in the Second World War? Most people don't know that – they should, but they don't."

"Is that right?" I said. "It's actually more the War in this part of London that I'm interested in."

"OK," Miss Brown said, "Well, there was, of course, a Somali community living in the docklands area during World War Two. Did you know that?"

"Actually, no. But if you could just tell me

some of the things that happened round here, that would be great."

Miss Brown opened her address book and ran a pencil down a list of names.

"I'll tell you who you should really speak to. Do you know Jan, the lollipop lady? She's quite a local historian. Knows all about the Blitz, which is what they called the fifty seven nights of bombing by the Nazis that started in September 1940."

I know more about the Blitz than you can possibly imagine, I thought, but all I said was, "Really?"

Miss Brown smiled encouragingly. "Anyway, Aisha, Jan's your woman. I've got her address and telephone number here, or you could catch her after school sometime."

She could see from the look on my face that I would probably be too shy to approach Jan. I knew the lollipop lady to smile at when I crossed the road, but I had hoped Miss Brown herself could tell me everything I wanted to know.

"There is a fair bit I can tell you," she added, "and there's lots in the library about the hardships the East End suffered. And, of course, our school here played a tragic role in it all."

I felt the skin tightening at my temples. I shook my head slowly. I tried to speak but no words came out. The fact that we were in a modern building, that Richard's Trentham School was all old and Victorian, I suppose these things had registered with me in the back of my mind somewhere, but if I'd thought anything, I'd just assumed they'd knocked the old place down at some point to build the new one.

"It wasn't hit by a bomb was it?" I asked weakly.

"I'm afraid it was. And a lot of local people who'd been bombed out of their homes were taking refuge there. It wasn't really a safe shelter for them and it took a direct hit. They don't even know for sure how many died, but several hundred people were inside and a lot of them were killed."

I closed my eyes tightly and willed myself back to Richard, but nothing happened.

"Are you all right, Aisha. Still suffering the effects of yesterday?"

"It's not that Miss Brown. It's to do with a really close friend of mine. Somehow, I've got to try and save him."

SUSPENDED

Mrs Greening wore a single metal earring, jagged like a piece of shrapnel, which dangled from her right ear. She was hunched over a computer keyboard with her back to us. A few intrepid sunrays crept into the room through a broken slat in the blinds, but the main source of light was a fluorescent tube above our heads, which buzzed like an angry insect. Mrs Greening swiveled slowly around in her chair to face us. Her dyed red hair was a bit like a clown's wig but shaved close around her neck and ears. Mrs Greening could be funny and kind but she was tough – at our school she had to be.

"Paperwork," she sighed. "I am drowning in paper."

Chevon smiled sympathetically as though she

understood the woes of a headteacher. I just looked past Mrs Greening's ear at a poster on her wall. I suppose this was something of a role reversal: me appearing all sullen and difficult; Chevon trying hard to be pleasant and polite.

"So," Mrs Greening said. "What am I going to do with you two? Any ideas?"

I shrugged. This was all such a waste of time. Someone I cared about had probably been blown to pieces in a real war and I was about to be disciplined over a fight in a school playground. I couldn't take the situation seriously but it seemed Chevon could. She spoke quietly and slowly as though she was thinking really hard about every word that left that pouty mouth of hers.

"We deserve to be punished for fighting and that," she said. "I know I come off worse, but it was my fault. I ain't been very kind to her, innit Aisha?"

We were side by side, just a pace apart, but I didn't even bother to turn and look at her.

Mrs Greening took some nicotine gum from a drawer in her desk and popped it into her mouth: she was always trying to give up smoking. She chewed thoughtfully.

"Well, this is something of a breakthrough for you, Chevon. I honestly can't remember the last time you took responsibility for anything."

"I just want to say that I'm sorry to Aisha for what I done in the past. I hope she can forgive me."

It was turning into one of those TV shows where they all kiss and make up. Mrs Greening looked at me over her glasses.

"Aisha?"

I shook my head. "Whatever," I whispered.

A little storm cloud passed over Mrs Greening's features.

"That is the sort of attitude I usually expect from Chevon, not you. Perhaps we could try again."

The strip light droned. Chevon swayed from side to side slightly as though she was listening to a slow song on headphones. Mrs Greening flicked some crumbs from the front of her blouse.

"Yeah, we can make up, if that's what Chevon wants. She's made my life here a misery though." I sighed wearily. "But if she wants to make up, I'll make up."

Mrs Greening gave a kind of half-smile. "Thank you, Aisha. I'm pleased to hear that."

Chevon coughed. "Was you still planning to expel us, Mrs Greening?" she asked in a sweetly anxious voice.

Mrs Greening chewed on her gum. "Not expel, Chevon. But I do plan to suspend you both until the end of the week. We can't have cat fights in school, can we? Miss Miles will type up a letter for you each to take home explaining the situation. Do you have anything else you'd like to say?"

It seemed there was no stopping Saint Chevon.

"Just that I'm really sorry to you Mrs Greening and to Aisha. It won't happen again."

I turned to face her and my eyes narrowed. Chevon, sincere? I didn't think so. Manipulative more like.

"Be honest. This is just an act because you're scared of being expelled. And after what happened in the classroom, you're scared of me."

Chevon looked confused and uncertain what to say. Mrs Greening answered for her.

"I think you'll find, Aisha, that the best policy is to move on. I don't know what you two have said to each other in the past, but it's time to put all that behind you. If you don't, you will have me to deal with."

I looked at the gauze bandage on Chevon's neck. It was grimy and a spot of blood had seeped through its centre.

"Mrs Greening," I said, "Chevon can't hurt me anymore. I've got much bigger problems in my life than Chevon."

Mrs Greening raised an eyebrow. "We can all behave like victims, Aisha. We just have to struggle on and make the best of life, don't you think?"

"Yes Mrs Greening." I stared blankly at her. I knew a smile would have helped but I just couldn't force one.

There were no smiles at home when I handed over the letter. My mother couldn't read it but she knew that official-looking documents usually contained bad news. As I related the conversation with Mrs Greening, Mum sat on our stained brown sofa. I stood before her defiantly.

"It's not like it's a surprise. You knew they'd suspend me."

"This is a terrible day. A terrible, terrible day."

"So you keep saying."

She pursed her lips and squinted at me. I knew she was angry as well as upset, but I wasn't ready for the bombshell that she was about to drop on me. "I'm glad your father didn't live to see this."

I burst into tears. Great hot salty drops ran down my cheeks and into the corners of my mouth. Why didn't she just slap me round the face? That pain would have been much easier to bear.

"I can't believe you said that," I stammered finally. "My father loved me."

"And because he loved you, he would have been destroyed by the way you shame him now."

I thought of my father and remembered a man with the widest smile, the whitest teeth and the most sparkly, smiley brown eyes. I remembered when the life was extinguished from those eyes by a gunman with a baseball cap turned backwards on his head and a crescent-shaped scar down one cheek. My father was just another statistic in Somalia's civil war. His death wasn't written up in any newspaper or announced on television. But he had been my heart's joy and when his life was snuffed out I felt my world would be grey forever.

"Your father wouldn't recognize you," she

went on. "He would want you to be a good Somali girl."

My legs had been feeling as if they might no longer hold my weight, but a jolt of anger went through me like electricity and though I still felt weak my mind was suddenly clear.

"And what is a good Somali girl exactly? Everything's changed, Mum. We're here now and everything is different. I refuse to be a victim any more. If there's one thing I've learnt, it's that. This world is full of victims. I'm looking at one right now. My own mother, the victim. But I'm not going to be a victim. I won't let you or anyone drag me down."

It seemed that the emotion had drained her. She just slumped on the sofa: a small woman lying back against the cheap cushions. Part of me felt sorry for her but I wanted to hurt her too. And I knew how to do it. I tilted my head back and jutted out my jaw. "By the way, I've got a new friend and he happens to be a boy."

"What do you mean?" she whispered.

"He's someone I feel very strongly about. A boy I feel very strongly about."

OK, so Richard was a boy who had lived and probably died more than sixty years ago. I still couldn't bring myself to admit that he was dead, but in any case I didn't care about mere details right now. He was real enough to me.

"What sort of a boy?"

"He isn't Somali if that's what you mean."

"I just meant..." Her words trailed off. She didn't know what she meant. "...I just find this all so hard to take, Aisha."

"Well get used to it because Richard is the most important thing in my life right now."

I wasn't prepared for the next bit. Instead of hitting me, my mum reached up and took me gently by the wrist.

"You don't look well, Aisha. Sit down before you fall."

Her tone had changed; her words were soothing. She pulled me towards her until we were sitting together on the sofa. I didn't resist.

I lay my head against her shoulder and let her stroke my hair. She was right, I thought, I wasn't well. I was sick to death of losing people.

BANG!

The local library was a modern chrome-and-glass building. Miss Brown, my teacher, had brought our class here once. We'd sat in the children's section on brightly-patterned scatter cushions under walls and ceilings splashed with cheerful colours. Today, though, everything was in black and white as I stared at one old photograph after another. If only the images could speak, I kept thinking, but they were fixed in time.

The young librarian seemed delighted that I hadn't just wanted to log on to the internet and look up song lyrics. Instead of asking me why I wasn't in school, he'd nodded seriously when I'd told him what I was after. He'd found websites and books and newspaper clippings.

I'd asked him for anything about the Blitz and our area, especially about the bombing of Trentham School. Of course, what I really wanted to discover was Richard's fate, though I knew in my heart it was probably a hopeless quest. I didn't even know Richard's surname. I suppose I was hoping that his cheeky face would just pop out from one of the photographs or from a picture in a news article.

"Found what you wanted?" the librarian whispered. His straw-coloured hair was thinning even though he didn't look that old.

I managed a weak smile. "Not yet. Thanks for all your help, though."

On the desk in front of me, he placed a file labelled 'History of Trentham School'. Some of the information inside dated back to the late 1800s. There were pictures of boys in Victorian collars all spruced up for the camera and little girls in clean white pinafore dresses. Behind them stood the soaring, three-storey, brick castle I'd seen that first day I met Richard. I shuddered when I came upon later photographs from the time of the Blitz. They showed the old school wrecked by the bomb – that dreadful direct hit – and scorched by fire. Firemen and others in wartime uniforms poked around in a wasteland of rubble and charred timbers, apparently looking for survivors.

In one picture a group of children stood to one side, but they were turning away from the photographer, their faces blurred. Could Richard have been one of them? Might he have survived after all? The newspaper clippings gave me little room for hope. It seemed that as many as three hundred people had died in the tragedy: their own homes destroyed already by bombs, they'd been killed while they sheltered in the school. The official death toll was not quite so high but the authorities had quickly abandoned the search of the wreckage – with further waves of Nazi planes on the way, there was little time to spend looking for the dead.

I read everything. The same phrases started

repeating themselves: "terrible tragedy", "defenceless women and children", "direct hit". The words went round and round in my head until I couldn't take any more.

I'd just decided to put everything back into the file when I saw a recent cutting from the local newspaper. It showed the modern-day version of Trentham School with the headline *Lollipop lady keeps wartime memories alive*. It was Jan, the woman Miss Brown had suggested I speak to. She was dressed in her lollipop lady's uniform but instead of the stick she usually held she was holding a wreath of flowers. I realized

there was something about her face that captivated me. I tried to close the file but I couldn't stop staring at her picture. With a shiver, I suddenly felt the strangest sensation that she would be able to tell me about Richard – that one way or another I would find out what had become of him.

★ ★ ★

I was desperate for Monday to arrive so that I could return to school – suspension over – and talk to Jan. My mum made me go shopping with her. She dawdled in and out of the pound shops on Green Street looking for cheap stuff she claimed we needed. I waited outside impatiently.

"What do you think of this tablecloth?" my mum asked from a doorway. The shop owner eyed her suspiciously as though she might try to flee with his junk.

"It's a tablecloth," I said. I knew I should try to be nicer, but my heart was heavy and I had no interest in such petty things.

"I'll leave it," she said and disappeared back into the depths of the shop.

I thought of staying in bed on Sunday but mum was crashing around in the kitchen as though the pots and pans were percussion instruments that needed a good work-out.

I reached for the picture of my dad that stood on a cabinet in a small silver-coloured frame. I brought it close, kissed the cold glass and held it tightly to my chest.

"Please let Richard have survived," I murmured. "I can't bear to lose him as well as you."

I looked at my father's smiling face. I knew that if he had any beyond-the-grave influence he would find a way to help me.

Finally, finally, Monday came and my mother was surprised to see me enthusiastic about leaving the house. She begged me to eat something before I left and I did manage a few mouthfuls, but my heart was pounding and the porridge tasted of nothing.

"I've got to go," I insisted.

"You will make yourself ill again," she

complained.

At last I was out of the door and running along the litter-strewn street. It was raining, a slanty sort of rain that whipped into my face, and the pavement was slick with liquid London grime. I almost toppled over a woman pushing a double pram: identical twins stared blankly at me from beneath a plastic rain sheet.

"Hey, careful!" she shouted as we swerved around each other.

"Sorry!" I called over my shoulder.

I turned the next corner, past the post box, and the school came into view. I was still a minute or so away, but, with a thrill, I realized that the dot in the yellow raincoat outside the gates was Jan. She was in her usual place, lollipop stick in hand. I was wheezing for breath but I pushed on, past groups of little kids who took up the width of the pavement with their brightly-coloured rucksacks and older ones who walked with a slow swagger, in no hurry at all.

At last I was at the crossing point opposite the

school. Jan had just escorted some children across the road. As she turned I could see a strand of blonde hair that had fallen loose from under her hat. She wiped her wet forehead and planted the lollipop stick in front of her as if she was a shepherd walking with a crook. Our eyes met. She had the kind of sparkly eyes I like. Elated, I stepped off the curb and into the road.

"Can I talk to you?" I started to call out.

But I saw fear flash in her eyes and her head seemed to twitch. "Get back!" she screamed.

I just froze, confused. All I could think about was getting across the road to her.

"Get back!" she shouted again.

It was then I became aware of the van. I sensed it as much as saw it, lurching at me all dirty and white. The driver was trying to brake and I heard the screeching sound of tyre rubber on a wet road.

I took a single pace back towards the safety of the pavement, which was enough to stop me being hit full on by the bonnet. Time seemed to stop somehow and for a moment I felt relieved. This stupid van was just a momentary inconvenience. Soon I would be talking to Jan about the Blitz and the old Trentham School and, above all, Richard. But even though she had saved me from stepping right in front of the speeding vehicle, I hadn't retreated quite far enough. The edge of the wing mirror clipped the side of my head and before I'd really had time to register any shock or pain or anything, I was once again falling through blackness, eyes tight shut.

A GHOSTLY LANDSCAPE

My feet were wet and numb with cold. I seemed to be standing in a small stream. It gurgled around me and lapped at my ankles. I opened my eyes and discovered I was in the middle of a cobbled yard that was awash with water from a broken pipe. In one corner was a wooden cart, laden with empty bottles, which had the words 'Direct Milk Supply' painted along its side. A man in a blue-and-white striped apron was leaning against the cart smoking a cigarette. The water from the burst water main bubbled over his boots, but he ignored it, concentrating instead on the rings of smoke that he blew into the air above his head.

I splashed happily across the yard towards him. Everything about him – his clothes, his wire-framed glasses, his haircut — told me what I wanted to know. I was back in 1940.

"Good morning, Mister Milkman," I called out breezily.

But he paid no more attention to me than to the water. I nudged the rickety cart and the empty milk bottles clinked together. He turned his head slightly, one eye half closed, but continued to form his smoke rings as carefully and thoughtfully as any artist.

"You can't see me, can you Mister Milkman?" I shouted, just inches away from him now. He had a handsome face, pale and with high cheekbones. From behind the small round glasses, his forget-me-not blue eyes stared right through me.

"I'm back!" I cried out to the milkman, to the world, to anyone who was listening. But nobody could hear me.

My elation soon evaporated when I stepped out of the yard and into the wasteland beyond. It seemed the dairy was one of the few buildings

left standing. But where exactly was I?

I picked my way through a wilderness of bricks. Charred trees poked up at intervals, their branches draped with curtain material and ripped-up strips of wallpaper. I followed the sound of scraping shovels. Someone was shifting broken glass and rubble behind a tall bomb-damaged wall on which was painted *Swan Vestas -- the Smoker's Match*. A smile flickered on my lips as I thought of the milkman and his smoke rings, but it was extinguished by the anxiety growing inside me. There were no landmarks I recognized to guide me back to Trentham School. It suddenly struck me that a big disadvantage of being a ghost from the future was that I couldn't ask anyone for directions.

I trudged through an eerie, desolate landscape for what felt like hours. People were clearing up the damage caused by earlier bombing raids and bracing themselves for the next attacks. Many of those I passed were like ghosts themselves. I saw a nurse in a spotless white uniform crouching down beside an old man whose face was engrained with soot. A barefoot woman in a green dressing gown was pacing in front of her house carrying a dented saucepan. I saw scruffy children, some around Richard's age, looking for souvenirs amidst the collapsed buildings. "What I really want is a bit of a German plane," said one.

I turned a corner and almost collided with a man so tall and thin he seemed to have been stretched. He wore a hat and a smart suit and in his lapel was a red rose that looked freshly picked. Richard would have said he was sticking up two fingers to Hitler with that flower. The man carried a case for a trumpet. Only when he was gone did I realize that he was black-skinned like me.

All the time it was getting darker and still I was lost. Cars drove past, their headlamps almost covered by tape so that thin shafts of light were all that lit their way. I saw that the traffic lights were covered up too. In the gathering gloom I found I was able to make out a sign on the building in front of me: *Rees's Dairy*.

I was back where I'd started.

My feet ached; my heart ached too. I was ready to sit down on the cracked pavement with my head in my hands when I saw a church looming up like a ship from a sea of rubble. Part of its roof was ripped away but outside was a handwritten notice. It read, *Open as usual*! It seemed such a cheerful note to strike in all this adversity. God only knows what my mum would have said, but I decided to go in.

It was dark inside the church and getting darker because the priest was blowing out all the candles. He was a kindly-looking man with a comical haircut that he'd surely fashioned himself. There were wispy silvery bits at the back that his scissors had apparently missed.

As he busied himself about the church I could see the crinkly laughter lines beside his eyes and it made me like him all the more. He was half humming, half singing a song about the 'Queen of the May', which seemed all wrong for a number of reasons – first off the Blitz had begun in September, second, the tune seemed far too happy. He paused thoughtfully before a statue of a woman dressed in a light blue robe and a white headscarf. I took her to be the Virgin Mary. The priest bent his head and said a little prayer or something under his breath then moved on to put out more candles, singing softly all the while.

Finally, he moved towards the side aisle where I was sitting. I noticed that he had a slight limp and, in the darkness, I saw him wince as he bowed towards the altar at the front of the church. It was weird that he'd chosen the same bench as me. Instinctively, I shuffled a little further down it, but he hobbled along until he was just a foot away from me, then, gripping the pew in front for support, he lowered himself down with a deep sigh. I slouched lower in my seat. OK, so I was invisible, but I still felt uncomfortable with him that close.

"You seem lost," he whispered.

I sat up with a start. It sounded like he was talking to me.

"You can see me?" I asked, wide-eyed.

"I have a knack for spotting people who are in pain. I'm Father Mackenzie."

"Aisha is my name," I replied. "And you're right, I am in pain. I'm worried about a friend of mine. I think he may be dead. I've been walking around for ages trying to find him – and a school called Trentham Primary. But I can't."

"Have you tried praying?"

I slid a few inches further along the smooth wooden pew.

"Don't think you're going to convert me. I'm a Muslim. I only came in here because I was exhausted and I'd given up hope of finding my friend."

Father Mackenzie smiled. "There are many paths that lead to the same place. I'm not sure my boss would agree with me but I think we all pray to the same God. And it's not just about your friend is it? I sense you carry a heavy burden of loss with you, Aisha."

I don't quite know where it all came from, but suddenly I was like that burst water pipe at the dairy, all bubbling up with tears.

"I lost my dad," I sobbed. "He was shot dead."

"In France?"

I looked across at him confused. "No, not in this war. In Somalia," I said.

He looked a little puzzled but his eyes were still warm and concerned. I was about to ask him to draw me a map of how to get to Trentham School, but I realized there were other things I wanted to know too.

"You believe in your religion that we'll see our loved ones again, right?"

He nodded. "Yes, we believe that."

"I hope it's true. Because I can't stand the thought that I'll never see my dad again."

Hot tears were spilling out of my eyes. I could actually hear the splash of them as they hit the stone floor even though I was coughing and spluttering too.

"But you see him every day don't you?" Father Mackenzie said. "Every time you look in the mirror. You carry him with you and that never goes away. To be honest, I didn't get on particularly well with my own father, but the older I get the more I see I'm turning into him. Right down to the hair that's started sprouting out of my ears."

Despite myself, I laughed and the sound echoed round the empty church. "Thanks, Father Mackenzie, but I want more than that."

He scratched his chin thoughtfully. "That's where faith comes in."

We sat in silence for a while, then I found I had to ask him something else. "Do you believe in ghosts?"

He didn't seem at all surprised. "I believe there are more things in heaven and earth than we can even dream of let alone explain. Are you a ghost then, Aisha?"

I turned the palms of my hands over and looked at them. "I don't think so. I'm from the future, where I'm properly alive and people can touch me and talk to me. But here, in the past, nobody can do that. Apart from my friend Richard. And now you."

He chuckled. "So you're from the future and right now you're in the past which, of course, is my present."

"That's confusing."

"It certainly shows how little we understand about time and how it works."

Suddenly I felt the strangest goose-pimply sensation. I'd seen that Bruce Willis film *The Sixth Sense*, where he doesn't realise he's a ghost. Maybe Father Mackenzie had been killed in the Blitz that very day and was just mooching around doing his normal priestly routine, not knowing he was actually dead.

"You're not a ghost are you?" I stuttered. "I mean, you haven't been killed by a bomb and you're just hanging around your church?"

Father Mackenzie looked a little taken aback. "I'm not dead yet thank you very much."

But even as he said it, he reached up a hand and touched his cheek as if to assure himself that he really did still exist.

A woman with wavy copper-coloured hair and a heavy woollen coat had come into the church and was making her way across to where we sat.

"Hello there, Father," she said.

I had to admit that, unless this woman was dead too, Father Mackenzie was still in the land of the living.

"I'll be with you in a minute, Anne," he called to her.

She wafted over to a small shrine where there were some tired-looking flowers and began to rearrange them. Father Mackenzie turned back to me.

"Before you go, I'll give you this."

He produced a pen and a piece of card. As he wrote and drew upon it, he poked the tip of his tongue out of the side of his mouth as though this work required a great effort of concentration. When he had finished, he nodded, then handed it to me.

"This should help you find your way," he said with a wink.

I took the piece of card and saw that he had mapped out a route for me from his church to Trentham School.

"How far is it?" I asked.

"About four or five miles, I should say. You'd best get going."

"Thank you for this. And for your words of wisdom."

"Oh, I've got plenty of them, don't you worry," he said with a twinkle in his eyes. "My advice to you, Aisha, would be to keep the memory of your father and the past alive. And in the future why don't you spend some time fixing things with your mother?"

My mouth just gaped open. "How do you know about my mum?"

He beamed at me. "Like I say, I have a sixth sense about people in pain."

How spooky is that? I thought for a second.

But as I emerged from the darkness of the church into a world already lit by the first flares and fires of a new bombing raid, I knew there was no time for reflection. That would have to wait. For now, I had to follow the flames. I had to keep going east.

SAVE YOURSELF!

I gripped the piece of card the priest had given me and stumbled on through a hell on earth. The deep bass boom of the bombs was joined by the inane clanging of fire-engine bells and the banshee wail of the sirens. I saw a pub spewing orange flames through its door as if it were a raging monster. I saw a factory that throbbed and glowed as though a fireball was trapped inside.

Everywhere firemen were climbing ladders, working pumps, running with fire hoses. I saw them silhouetted against the night sky trying to douse the blazes on every street. The choking smell of smoke and burning rubber made any currents of fresher air taste all the sweeter.

I walked along a main road beside a group of air raid wardens who were using a door as a

makeshift stretcher for an injured colleague. The man kept insisting he was all right, but the bandages on his legs were drenched in blood. As the wardens ran they shouted at anyone not in uniform who loitered in their path. "Don't just stand there gawping. Get away from here!"

Eyes once more on my map, I turned a corner on to a stretch of open grass and stopped. Above me was a huge lumbering barrage balloon, meant to repel the war planes. It thrashed and rolled against its moorings like a giant white elephant. I walked on a few paces until a skinny black dog made me halt once more. It tore out from behind a bush and began barking wildly. At first I thought it had seen me or at least sensed my presence, but it was simply crazed with terror.

I could feel my heart pounding in my chest, but I felt excited as well as afraid now. The going was much easier on the scrubland and I was getting closer all the while. I could feel it.

Then I saw the sweep of a railway

embankment ahead of me, and my heart leapt into my throat. Once I'd climbed that slope, I'd be able to see the school, if it was still standing. What if I reached the summit of the hill and there was no three-storey castle on the horizon? What if the old Trentham School was in flames or had been bombed flat already? I realised that the longer it took me to scale the embankment, the longer I could keep the dream of Richard alive.

I slipped on some loose earth and suddenly I was flat on my back. I lay there for a few seconds, panting and glaring up at the sky which had rained so much destruction. Richard didn't deserve to die. He was just a young boy, a kind boy, a boy who'd seen the best in me. He'd told me that I was worth something, that there was a place for me in this world once the bombing stopped.

I felt overcome with anger for the people who start wars: the powerful people whose thirst for still more power is never satisfied; the man with the dirty baseball cap and the crescent-shaped scar who'd enjoyed his little bit of power when he gunned down my father. As I lay there, I realized I couldn't conjure up the gunman's face any more, but I remembered my father's face. I would keep my father's memory alive and Richard's memory too if it came to that.

I staggered to my feet. The sky above the embankment was red like a sunset. Just ahead of me was a wire fence behind which curved the railway track. As I reached the summit, I grabbed the fence in both hands, paused, then shrieked with delight. There in front of me stood Richard's school, looking more like a castle than ever. The bombs falling on the docks beyond it were suddenly a glorious firework display. Richard still lived.

It was easy now. I would have walked barefoot across shards of glass to get to that school. I scampered along streets that looked weirdly familiar even though they were missing the off-licenses and convenience stores I knew.

Nothing could stop me now. Once I'd explained how much danger he was in, Richard would leave the school, go back to his railway arch and be saved.

As I reached the playground, I saw a huge bomb crater that extended from just inside the gate to the wall of the school. It was filled with muddy water. A near miss.

The building itself was dark, with boards and black curtains up at the windows, but I knew there were people inside. I heard babies crying and mothers singing softly. A man's drunken voice was shouting, apparently at the Nazi bombers. "Why don't you come down here? I'll fight the lot of you." Despite myself, I laughed.

I walked down an empty, echoing corridor, feeling my way in the darkness along the smooth, cold wall. The classroom doors I passed were closed but I could hear snatches of conversation. From one room came the sound of a dreadful snoring. "For God's sake shut him up, can't you?" someone was complaining. I just knew that snore could belong to one person only: Richard's grandad. And if he was there, Richard must be close by. I gripped the small gold-coloured doorknob and twisted it. The decibel level of the snoring increased to that of a road drill.

"If I wake him up, you'll have to listen to him talking. And that'd be even worse. Trust me."

It was a boy's voice, a sweet voice.

I watched his silhouette pick its way carefully over the sleeping forms on the floor. Finally he was standing in front of me with a lopsided grin and that mass of hair all curled up on itself.

"You came back then?"

There was so much I wanted to say to him, but I knew the bomb, the direct hit, might come that very night. I had to convince him to leave the school now before it was blown to smithereens.

"Richard, you're in terrible danger. You've got to leave."

"Leave?" he said, his eyes smiling reassuringly.

"We've barely just got here."

I didn't know how to explain it all to him. "The thing is..." I started, then stopped, then started again. "The thing is, I know that this school is going to be hit by a massive bomb and maybe hundreds of people are going to be killed."

"What do you mean, *maybe hundreds will be killed?*"

"Well they don't know how many, cos they called off the search. But lots of people will die and you'll be one of them if we don't go now."

Richard looked troubled, but he wasn't freaking out or anything. "How do you know this, Aisha?"

"Because I'm from the future. I know everything that's going to happen."

He rolled his lower lip thoughtfully. "So who wins the war?"

"We do," I said.

"That's good," he said. But he seemed distracted. "And will West Ham ever win the league?"

I was getting angry with him now. I was trying to save his life and all he could think about was football.

"Will they, Aisha?" he persisted. "It's important to me."

"I don't know Richard. I don't really follow football. I think they've won some things, but even people who support them are always moaning about them."

He laughed and put his hand on my shoulder. "You're funny, Aisha."

"I'm serious. You've got to leave here now. And you've got to convince as many people as possible to leave with you."

Richard shrugged wearily. "How can I convince them to do that? They've been bombed out of their homes. I know this place isn't really any safer, but to them it feels like it is. It's like a castle. It doesn't look like you could knock it down."

"Richard, please. It will be knocked down. It will be a tomb for these people, your grandad included. You said you wanted to keep an eye on him. If no one else will go, at least wake him up and take him with you."

"Aisha, you're a great girl and I'm really grateful to you..."

I grabbed his hand and yanked it hard. "I've got to save you, Richard. You mean such a lot to me."

He winced, then flexed his fingers gingerly as though I'd really hurt him.

"I'll have a chat with my grandad cos I can see

this is important to you. But to be honest, I doubt I'll even be able to wake him. He can sleep through anything. Maybe in the morning things will look different."

This was just not going as I'd planned. I was desperately thinking of a way to make him see sense when he raised his hand again and touched the side of my face.

"I'll talk to him, Aisha. I'll talk to him in the morning."

I reached out to him once more but I suddenly felt the weirdest sensation. We were drifting apart. I felt weightless, like a leaf on a river. I could see Richard standing before me, but he was getting smaller and smaller as though he was at the opening of a tunnel and I was falling backwards down it, slowly but steadily, like Alice down the rabbit hole on her way to Wonderland.

"Please save yourself!" I called back to him.

But my voice was just a tiny, wispy thing like the head of a dandelion when it's turned to seed.

I tried to shout once more and felt something damp and cool press down on my forehead.

"I think she's trying to talk," said a voice I didn't recognise.

I opened one eye. Everything was white: the sheets, the pillows, the curtain round the bed.

"You've been in a coma," said my mother.

A PREMONITION

It didn't take too long for me to get back on my feet, but I wasn't allowed out of the hospital until I'd had about a million tests. My mum was with me all the time and for once that didn't feel suffocating: it felt good. I thought about what Father Mackenzie, the priest, had said about fixing things with her and I could see it starting to happen already.

Mum told me that Jan the lollipop lady had visited me while I'd been unconscious. This was nice to know in one way, but really annoying in another. It seemed I was destined not to talk to her. Of course, I was still burning with questions about the bombing of the old school and I still had this weird feeling she would be able to tell me about Richard's fate.

At last, I was well enough to go and visit her. My teacher Miss Brown, who'd been really concerned about me, had rung to fix everything.

I went round to Jan's house on a wet, blustery day, not unlike the one when I'd had my accident. I took a bunch of flowers with me, lilies, which Miss Brown said were classy and which she loved to receive herself.

The house looked well cared for and the front gate, unlike most of the ones on the street wasn't hanging off its hinge. I clicked it shut behind me and walked up the path. When I pressed the bell, it played a cheerful tune and within seconds Jan was at the door, all smiles and welcome and blonde hair scraped back in a ponytail.

"Look who it is," she said. "How're you feeling now, darling?"

She showed me in to a small lounge with a TV in one corner and a table with a pretty red and white tablecloth by the door to the kitchen.

"These lilies are gorgeous. My favourite," she confided as she disappeared into the kitchen in search of a vase.

I sat down on one of the chairs at the table and we chatted through the doorway about the accident and the blow to my head. I told her that I might have been killed if she hadn't screamed at me to go back. She said it was best not to think about such things and to try and put them behind you. To tell the truth, I was feeling a bit awkward because I wasn't in the mood for small talk. I just wanted to quiz her about the war and Trentham School.

Finally, she brought up the subject herself. "Miss Brown tells me you're really interested in the history of the Blitz and that?" she said, placing the lilies on the table between us. Their scent was almost overpowering.

"I really am," I said. "Specially the bombing of the school."

Jan nodded. "A terrible tragedy. And it nearly meant that I was never born."

"Why's that?" I asked politely, but inside I was thinking, *What could it possibly have to do with you?*

"It's quite a story," she said, standing up again. "Do you want a drink? I was just making a tea for myself when you arrived. I've got a coke, or a juice if you like."

I told her I was fine and listened impatiently to the clatter of the mug and the spoon, and the clunk of the fridge door as she busied herself in the kitchen. Finally the kettle whistled, she made her tea and came back in to the lounge frowning slightly.

"Now where was I?"

"You were saying the tragedy at the school nearly meant that you weren't born."

"Well," she said. "My dad and his grandad were sheltering there because they'd been bombed out of their house. But my dad had a premonition that they should get out of there sharpish. They tried to get the other people to go too, but everyone thought they were mad. In the end the two of them were sleeping under an old railway arch when the bomb finally dropped on Trentham."

"So they were OK? They survived?" My heart was pounding hard and I felt faint. I moved further away from the lilies and their sickly smell.

"Yeah, they survived. And like I say, if my dad had stayed I wouldn't have been born.

She raised her eyebrows as though to say, *Imagine that!*

"What sort of a premonition was it?" I asked. "Did he ever say?"

She shook her head slowly and rolled her lower lip. "I don't know. He was always very cagey about that. Partly I suppose because he felt guilty he'd been spared when so many others died." She leaned across the table and grabbed a tissue from a box. "Are you alright, love?"

I was crying now. I could see she thought I must still be suffering from the accident. I blew my nose on the tissue she'd handed me.

'D'you mind if I ask your dad's name? It wasn't Richard, was it?'

She looked stunned. "How d'you know that?"

Wiping the tears away I carried on. "And did he have a happy life after the war?"

"Yeah, I would say so." Jan leant back in her chair. "But you don't have to take my word for it. If you hang on a few minutes you can ask him yourself. He's out walking the dog."

★ ★ ★

The clock ticked loudly on the wall as though it was linked to some package that was about to blow up. Finally I heard claws scratching against the front door. Then I heard a key in the lock. The door creaked open and I could hear a man stamping his feet on the mat and talking sweetly to the dog as he took off its lead.

He entered the room and I knew at once that it was Richard. He still had those spaghetti curls piled up on his head and those smiling eyes. He actually looked a lot like his wild old grandad.

"Well, who have we got here then?" he asked.

"Dad," Jan said. "I'd like you to meet Aisha."

He looked quite shocked for a moment, but he composed himself quickly.

"Aisha," he said, as though it was a name he'd known all his life. "Aisha from Somalia."

ABOUT THE STORY

Many people ask me about the real events that inspired *Ghostscape*. They want to know if I've taught Somali girls like Aisha in the schools where I've worked, and if Richard is based on my dad, who was growing up in the East End of London during the Second World War. Most of all, they ask if there really was a school like Trentham, destroyed during The Blitz and later rebuilt. The answer is yes.

On the night of 10th September 1940 several hundred people, made homeless by the bombs, were taking shelter in an East London school called South Hallsville. The school suffered a direct hit and at least 73 people – most of them children – were killed. Locals believe many more died but were never found in the rubble. A later bombing raid killed my dad's aunt and the four young cousins he played with, Patrick, Sheila, John and Roberta. These events have stayed with me, and they've made me remember that whenever there is war – in Britain, Somalia, wherever – children will be among the victims.

JOE LAYBURN has spent most of his life in East London. His dad thought it would be fantastic for Joe and his three brothers to grow up surrounded by the fresh air and green fields of the country but Joe missed London and moved back as soon as he could.

Joe was a TV reporter and journalist for 15 years before becoming a teacher. He has always loved writing stories. He based Aisha on the vibrant and fascinating Somali children he worked with in East London. Richard is based on Joe's father who lived in the East End for much of the Second World War, despite his aunt and cousins being killed in a bombing raid in 1942.

Joe lives in East London with his wife Marianne and three sons, Richie, Charlie, and Hal. Joe and his sons are season-ticket holders at West Ham football club. This is his first novel.

MORE FICTION FROM FRANCES LINCOLN CHILDREN'S BOOKS

Black and White

Rob Childs
Illustrated by John Williams

Josh is soccer-mad and can't wait to show off his
ball skills to his new classmates. After all, he is the
nephew of Ossie Williams – the best footballer
in the country.

Josh's arrival helps to give shy Matthew more confidence,
but it is not welcomed by Rajesh, the school goalkeeper
and captain. With important seven-a-side tournaments
coming up, will the players be able to settle their
differences and work together as a team?

Angel Boy

Bernard Ashley

When Leonard Boameh sneaks away from
home to do some sightseeing, little does he know
that his day out is about to turn sinister.
Outside Elmina Castle, the old fort and slave prison,
groups of street kids are pestering the tourists,
and before Leonard knows it, he is trapped
in a living nightmare.

Set in Ghana, this chilling chase
adventure is one you'll never forget.

From Somalia with Love

Na'ima B. Robert

Safia knows that there will be changes ahead but
nothing has prepared her for the reality of dealing
with Abo's cultural expectations, her favourite brother
Ahmed's wild ways, and the temptation of her cousin
Firdous' party-girl lifestyle. Safia must come to terms
with who she is — as a Muslim, as a teenager,
as a poet, as a friend, but most of all, as a daughter
to a father she has never known. Safia must find
her own place in the world, so both father and
daughter can start to build the relationship
they long for.

From Somalia, with Love is one girl's quest to
discover who she is — a story rooted in Somali
and Muslim life that will strike a chord
with young people everywhere.